PURNIMA

A SPIRITUAL FICTION SERIES

WALDMEER SERIES
BOOK 7

DONNA GODDARD

Second Edition 2023

Published by Donna Goddard

Victoria, Australia

Paperback ISBN: 978-0645729665

Large Print ISBN: 978-1764151153

Cover design by Donna Goddard

www.donnagoddard.com

CONTENTS

PART I

THE FIRST PASSAGE

PURNIMA PASSAGE

1. Seeing the Totality   5
2. Waldmeer Advancement Association   8
3. Buzz Beanie   10

TOM & HARDY

4. Woop Woop   15
5. Ekadashi   18
6. Kissing Nicely   20

ABANDON

7. Urgent and Confidential   25
8. Worth Wanting   27

PART II

PURNIMA AND POETRY

GUM FLAT

9. Running By   35
10. Night Train   37
11. Timeless   40

SAME SONG SUNG

12. Drunks and Bogans   47
13. Snake Pit   50
14. Third Eye   53

STILL POINT

15. Mr Peen's Fire   59
16. Purnima to Purnima   63
17. There the Dance Is   65

TWENTY MILE TRACK

18. Puddle Muddle   69
19. Lines and Loonies   71
20. Monthly Cycle   73

PART III
STONES OF SPRING

AUGUST ASHES

21. The Giant School Stalker   79
22. Temple Thief   82
23. Duos and Trios   84

STONE GROUND

24. Return of the Snakes   89
25. Rack and Ruin   91

RING OF SILVER

26. Go to the Monastery   95
27. Set Your Devotion   98

PART IV
KEEP ONLY THAT

HEALING RING

28. Sadhana   105
29. Washed Away with Tears   107
30. No One Came   110

FLAME

31. Made To Be Used   115
32. Feed and Burn   118

REBORN

33. Old-New   123
34. Blessed   125

WHAT WE MUST KEEP

35. Dark and Deep   129
36. Sunrise   131

PERFECT PURNIMA

37. Best Interest   137
38. Life Plays   139
39. Sweetheart   141
40. No Hands   143

Summary of Waldmeer Series   147
About the Author   149
Also by Donna Goddard   151

PART I
THE FIRST PASSAGE

PURNIMA PASSAGE

CHAPTER 1
SEEING THE TOTALITY

A full moon evening, late in May, in Waldmeer:

Purnima means full moon. Full moons are auspicious occasions for new beginnings, so we begin, again.

Merlyn and Gabriel stood awkwardly at the entrance of Twenty Mile Track. *Awkward* because they barely knew each other, and this seemed too big an adventure for virtual strangers. Nevertheless, there they were, brought together by some unknown force.

The force wasn't exactly unknown. It was Amira, after all, and she wasn't unknown. Gabriel certainly knew her. Knew her more than anyone else. Knew her until that night, a few months ago, when she left this world. It wasn't really *this* world that she left. At the time of her passing, Gabriel and Amira lived in the Great Valley of the inter-dimensional Borderfirma Mountains. So, she didn't leave Earth, but nor was she here, except for one place, Ajna Temple. But that was only known to Merlyn (and also Rybert, who, on Amira's instructions, had been told).

This evening was brought about by another of Amira's instructions. She recently told Merlyn that the entrance to Twenty Mile Track was a gateway to the inter-dimensional Stone Ground.

Stone Ground was a large, round rock balanced on a flat rock, next to the Borderfirma Lowlands palace. Amira's son, Aristotle, and his wife, Indra, lived in the palace. Just as Floating Cave Monastery was built around the sacred salt pond of Floating Cave, the Lowlands palace was built around the equally sacred and powerful rock structure, Stone Ground.

Indra had grown up in her father's house next to Floating Cave. She knew how to guard the etheric power sources. And Aristotle was part of the spiritual bloodline of Faith-Amira with his own gentle, intuitive, and loving nature. Gabriel had a lot to do with Aristotle when he was a child. He considered him partly as his own. That was a good considering.

Amira explained to Merlyn that every full moon, the grassy area at the beginning of Twenty Mile Track became an inter-dimensional passage for twenty-four hours. Then, it closed again until the next full moon. The portal was aptly called Purnima Passage. However, as far as Merlyn could tell, no one in Waldmeer or even Prana Community called it that. So, Merlyn wondered who the people were referring to it as Purnima Passage.

This full moon was a particularly special one. It was the Buddha Purnima that celebrates all things Buddha. However, of more widespread interest, it was also a red moon. In opposite parts of the sky, the moon would be getting ready to rise as the sun set.

The full moon normally passes below or above the

Earth's shadow. On red moon, it passes directly through the Earth's shadow, causing a lunar eclipse called *totality*. Instead of blacking out, the moon becomes red and puts on a show.

Merlyn heard the folk of Waldmeer talking about the red moon. She knew some were planning to take up a possie on the pier to witness the event. As Waldmeer's magnificent main beach faced east, the sunrises and moonrises were spectacularly unhampered. She hoped that none of them intended to come to Twenty Mile Track, which started a mere few streets behind the Waldmeer shops.

It's not particularly secret or hidden for an important energetic gateway, she thought.

Some things are best hidden by remaining directly in front of everyone's eyes.

CHAPTER 2
WALDMEER ADVANCEMENT
ASSOCIATION

A *few days ago, in Waldmeer:*
It had not been an easy matter to get Gabriel to meet Merlyn at Purnima Passage. A few days ago, Merlyn went to the Waldmeer Advancement Association and waited for Gabriel to finish the art class he was teaching there. Assuming she was a new student, he handed her an entry form.

"Umm, no, thanks," said Merlyn nervously. "I'm not here to enrol in the art classes."

Gabriel looked at her more intently and said, "Oh, I recognise you. You're Ide's friend from the Waldmeer Warriors dance classes. She told me about you. And I remember your face from when I was at Prana Community for Mahashivratri."

"Yes," said Merlyn, feeling partially relieved. "I know it sounds a little strange, but I have a message for you."

"From who?" asked Gabriel suspiciously.

"I'm sorry, I can't tell you," said Merlyn.

She knew that sounded pathetic. She wished Amira

would allow her to tell Gabriel the message was from her. It would make everything so much easier, but Amira had insisted that Gabriel could find her himself when he was ready.

"I don't take messages from anonymous people," said Gabriel, turning to leave.

"It's about Borderfirma," said Merlyn quickly.

Gabriel stopped walking and turned back to Merlyn. "Go on," he said.

"There is a gateway to Borderfirma at the entrance of Twenty Mile Track," said Merlyn. "It's only open once a month for twenty-four hours. I'm going to go, and I need a guide."

"No," said Gabriel. "Not me."

Feeling that there was nothing else she could do, Merlyn said, "I'll be there before moonrise."

CHAPTER 3
BUZZ BEANIE

Back to this evening at *Twenty Mile Track:*

While most Waldmeerians' eyes were on the eastern horizon and the red moon, Gabriel and Merlyn stared at the opening ball of light at the entrance of Twenty Mile Track. It was as big as a two-storey house.

"Seeing as we are both here," said Gabriel, forcing himself to put a foot into the glowing light of Purnima Passage, "we might as well go."

Merlyn hesitated and said, "I do have to be back by tomorrow evening. I'm starting a new job in Waldmeer."

"Where?" asked Gabriel.

"At the Waldmeer Warriors," said Merlyn. "Malik asked me if I would take over his wife's job at the desk, as she hasn't been well lately."

"I thought you lived out of town," said Gabriel. "It's a long drive."

"Yes, I've been living on Shambhavi and Veronica's property," said Merlyn, "but I decided to move back into town.

Malik told me the granny flat across the road from him is empty again."

It was the same flat that Merlyn had lived in last spring and some of summer. After she moved out to go to Prana Community, the owners had no trouble renting it to holiday-makers. Now that the weather was cold, they were happy to take a long-term renter again.

"I had two dogs," said Merlyn, "but not now."

"Sorry," said Gabriel.

Bella was put to sleep not long after moving to Shambhavi's. The vet told Merlyn she was a ripe old age for a cavalier. Normally, their predisposition to heart problems means that they don't get to have old-age problems, which Bella did have.

One afternoon, a few weeks after Bella's passing, Bertie, Merlyn's German shepherd, put his heavy paw in her lap and quietly closed his eyes for the last time. Merlyn knew he wanted to go. He was grateful for his happy time with her, but missed Bella and wanted to see his old mistress again. And he felt tired.

Not long after, Merlyn told Shambhavi that as she no longer had dogs, it would be best to move back to Waldmeer and take a job in town. He understood. It wasn't only the dogs.

Merlyn felt she was living a bit too close to someone else's marriage. He understood that, too. He did give her a parting gift—his electric shaver. It was just what she wanted. He knew that, too.

According to the tradition of Guru Gadubanud's monks in his Southern Indian ashram, Merlyn decided to shave her head. It was to be done the day before Purnima. She told Shambhavi her idea. In his customary, well-mannered way, he suggested she use his electric shaver guard, set to a reasonable length, instead of completely shaving it. Then she wouldn't be "too cold", which translated as *too bald*.

Merlyn took his advice and the shaver and now had a buzz cut, which she had ceremoniously performed alone in Ajna Temple according to the traditional rites. That is why she had a beanie on tonight, but Gabriel would have simply thought it was a cold night.

"If we don't hurry up, we won't be going anywhere," said Gabriel.

"You lead the way," said Merlyn. "You know what you are doing."

Gabriel wished that he did *know what he was doing*. Regardless, he reassuringly touched Merlyn's beanied head and stepped forward into the shimmering glow.

TOM & HARDY

CHAPTER 4
WOOP WOOP

In the Wurt Wurt Koort Tearooms:

I n the Wurt Wurt Koort Tearooms:

As planned, Merlyn returned to Waldmeer from Borderfirma before Purnima Passage closed. She spent the twenty-four hours in the Lowlands palace with Aristotle and Indra, trying to make sense of it all. When it was time to go back to Waldmeer, Gabriel told her to return without him and that he would come back next full moon as he had "stuff to sort" in Borderfirma.

As Merlyn was now part of the inner circle who knew of Borderfirma, and Rybert was another in that circle, she visited him the next day to talk about her inter-dimensional trip. He listened carefully and then told Merlyn that Tom wasn't coming to the Wurt Wurt Koort Tearooms anymore. Rybert didn't tell her that yesterday, on Purnima evening, while he and Tom were gazing at the full moon, they had their own little drama, which entailed a lot of swearing.

~

Yesterday at the Wurt Wurt Koort Tearooms:

"You know that I appreciate you coming to the tearooms to help me," Rybert said to Tom, "but why?"

"Why what?" asked Tom.

"Why are you still coming?" said Rybert. "I've been back home since the end of summer, and we are almost into winter."

Tom shrugged. Rybert knew that Tom's lack of engagement was an unwillingness to pursue the conversation, but he had already decided that he wanted to pursue it.

"It's not like you aren't busy in the city with your cafe," said Rybert. "What is it you get from coming here? I don't think you are that fond of me that you can't keep away."

He smiled, but Tom was still unengaged.

Rybert continued, "Is it someone else?"

Tom now looked at Rybert with eyes that said, *Stop talking, buddy.* Rybert didn't stop.

"Is it Merlyn?" said Rybert. "Is that why you were so hot under the collar about Merlyn and me?"

"That's fucking stupid," said Tom. "I don't feel like that about women."

"Do you feel like that about anyone?" persisted Rybert.

"Of course I do," said Tom. "You, of all people, know that."

"I know about me," said Rybert, "but I don't think you do. Know about yourself, that is. You avoid relationships. For sure, you can flirt your arse off, but you avoid real relationships with mastered precision. Essentially, you are flirting your life away."

"You're no better," said Tom tartly. "I don't see no lovers keeping you company in the middle of Woop Woop."

"No, Tom, you are wrong," said Rybert. "I am better. I am

better than that. I know what I am doing. You don't. My life is by choice. It's conscious dysfunction. You are unconscious dysfunction."

Tom didn't laugh at Rybert's joke. Instead, he said, "You know what? You are right. Why am I here?"

And that was the last Rybert saw of Tom.

CHAPTER 5
EKADASHI

Ten days later, in the city, at Tom & Hardy:

"You don't want any food today?" asked Tom. "Only coffee? Aren't you hungry, boo?"

"No, not really," said Merlyn as she leaned down to pat Tom's little dog, Hardy. "Anyway, it's Ekadashi."

"E-Kardashian?" said Tom.

Merlyn laughed and said, "Ekadashi, the 11th day after full moon. Guru Gadubanud said that we should fast. Usually, I don't deliberately fast. But I'm not hungry some days, so I don't eat much."

"What does the fasting do?" asked Tom.

"Rests the system," said Merlyn. "Resets the body."

Although Tom wasn't familiar with Ekadashi, he was a conscious eater. You only had to look at his body to see that, not a kilo of extra fat, lean muscle. He instinctively followed his body rhythm of eating only two meals a day, and those during the latter part of the day. He was essentially fasting his body every day.

Merlyn thought about the many bad habits people have

that support their unconscious eating. Eating while watching television was one. Eating while conversing with people was another. Although family dinners can be a good way for people to connect, they can also be the reason for a great deal of heartburn.

"I like eating alone," said Merlyn.

One of Tom's best qualities was that Merlyn could say any weird thing to him (and often did), and he never wrote it off as being stupid. He might make a joke, but then he put it in the back of his mind. Something not understood, but a possibility. A possibility. That made all the difference. He wasn't opinionated.

That is probably what made him good with lots of different people. He listened to their stories without giving his opinion unrequested.

CHAPTER 6
KISSING NICELY

After Tom took her order, Merlyn found a table, sat down, and removed her hat.

"I like your haircut," said Tom, placing her coffee down.

"I thought you would," said Merlyn.

Her buzz cut had nearly two weeks of growth to soften it. Tom looked at Merlyn's clothes as she took off her coat.

"Why have you got dancing clothes on?" asked Tom. "I thought you were here to see me?"

"I am here to see you," said Merlyn. "But I'm also going next door to the State Ballet for a class while I'm in the city."

Tom rolled his eyes.

"I'm only here once a week," said Merlyn. "It's a long drive from Waldmeer."

"Whatever," said Tom. "I don't really like your hair. I lied."

"Oh, right," said Merlyn. "I thought you'd like it because...."

"Because what?" said Tom caustically. "Because you look like a boy?"

Merlyn supposed that that was probably correct.

"I'm a traditionalist," said Tom irrationally. "Long hair on girls. Short hair on boys."

Merlyn screwed up her face and thought, *Traditionalist? What in God's name is he talking about?* After a moment, she concluded, *He has a high level of jealousy for a low level of what he is willing to offer.*

The Tom & Hardy toilet walls were filled with Thomas Hardy quotes. They were all pasted on, along with magazine pictures, to make a messy sort of billboard effect. Merlyn wondered how many people sat there too long, thinking about the quotes, while a queue assembled outside the door. Tom said his favourite one was:

You ride well, but you don't kiss nicely at all.

— T. HARDY

Then, he would wink and strut off. Today, there was neither kissing nor winking nor strutting. Merlyn decided to leave and warm up early for her dance class.

ABANDON

CHAPTER 7
URGENT AND CONFIDENTIAL

M id-June in Waldmeer:
It was late morning before there was enough sun for Merlyn to sit outside her small rented flat. She sat there doing nothing, thinking nothing, staring at the sea below. This spot was the only place she could see the ocean from her home. It was worth sitting in the cold—coat, beanie, scarf, and gloves.

Anyway, cold or not, being outside always seems to change our perspective. It changes things that can best do with a change. The wind dismantles the heaviness, the light reorients the mind, the greenness invigorates hope, and the entire majestic dynamic of nature reminds us of our insignificance and also of our absolute significance.

Eventually, Merlyn checked her emails and read one from Prana Community marked *Urgent and Confidential.*

Dear Prana Community members,

We regret to inform you that there has been a death in Prana Community early this morning. A body was found in Ajna Temple, next to the linga. We believe it is local resident Gabriel, who may be known to some of you.

He lived in Waldmeer for many years, then was away for twenty years, and recently returned and started art classes at the Waldmeer Advancement Association. He has been residing in the home of another long-time Waldmeer resident, Ide.

As the cause of death is unknown, and Gabriel was a healthy sixty-year-old with no known medical issues, the police have marked it as needing further investigation.

A small brown bottle was discovered next to his body. It has a label—*Property of Floating Cave Monastery.*

The police have asked anyone who knows about Floating Cave Monastery to come forward. No one here has heard of it.

We extend our deepest sympathies to all who knew Gabriel.

Sincerely, Prana Community Board

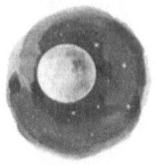

CHAPTER 8
WORTH WANTING

T he next day, in the Wurt Wurt Koort Tearooms:
"You aren't going to the police, are you?" asked Merlyn.

"Of course not," said Rybert. "What did Gabriel say to you before you left him in Borderfirma?"

"He said he would stay for a while with Aristotle and Indra and then walk the day to Floating Cave Monastery. He said he liked it there, and the monk was an old friend. He also said that one of his all-time favourite places was the salt pond of Floating Cave. Then he was going to walk another day to Odin's cottage in the Great Valley. Aristotle told Gabriel that no one had been there since his mother's death, so the forest had probably taken over the house. Gabriel said that it didn't matter."

After some time, Rybert said, "He must have worked out that it was Amira who told you about Purnima Passage being a gateway to Borderfirma. It was only one step from you to Prana Community. And one more step to Ajna Temple and Amira."

"He was strong and well," said Merlyn. "He probably had another thirty years left in him. How would he have died?"

"The monk has countless bottles of potions in the monastery," said Rybert. "Who would know what they are for? Perhaps Gabriel did know. I'm not accusing the monk of giving Gabriel the bottle, but maybe Gabriel took it."

"The moon is still growing. It's another week till Purnima Passage opens again," said Merlyn. "How would he have got back here?"

"He might have used the frame, the one in Odin's cottage," said Rybert. "The one that brought him back to Waldmeer a few months ago and also brought Maria, Odin, and me back."

"But why?" asked Merlyn. "I don't get it. Gabriel could have had a life in Borderfirma. He could have had a life here on Earth."

Rybert walked around the room, picking up a few things.

Eventually, he said, as much to himself as to Merlyn, "That's what happens with someone like Amira. When she first enters your life, you are so ignorant. You think you are smart. Smart enough to work out that she has something worth wanting. And you think that all you have to do is get her to love you. And wham—you're in!"

Rybert laughed at the thought, laughed at the ignorance of it, and laughed because it was more pleasant to laugh than cry.

"Foolish," he chastised. "Amira lets you continue with your thoughts because she doesn't want you to lose momentum. In the early stages, it is very connected to your attachment to her. As time goes along, you realise that it isn't working how you thought. She doesn't do what you want. In fact, the whole thing seems to be causing more pain than anything else. In disgust, you decide to abandon ship. But, I'm afraid, it's too late."

"Too late to abandon ship?" asked Merlyn.

"No," said Rybert. "You can abandon ship. But it doesn't help. It's too late. You are stuck in the middle. Can't go backward. Can't go forward. The middle is not an easy place to be."

"Why can't you go back?" asked Merlyn.

"Normal life isn't enough anymore," said Rybert. "It will never be enough again. You have crossed the line."

"Well, why can't you just keep going forward?" asked Merlyn.

"In theory, you can," said Rybert. "But it's hard. It takes a lot of effort. Amira does her best to help, but we must do it ourselves. We have to want it and understand it. So, she waits. She won't go away. Once the process has started, she won't abandon ship, no matter how many times we do."

"I still don't understand," said Merlyn.

Rybert looked at Merlyn's genuine face and said, "Gabriel lived with her too long."

Merlyn realised that there was no point questioning Rybert any further on the matter, and it was probably something that would become clearer to her with time.

However, she did ask one more, different question, "Where is Gabriel now?"

"That, I don't know," said Rybert.

"I went to the temple yesterday afternoon after reading the email," said Merlyn.

"And?" asked Rybert.

"It's not only Gabriel who has gone," said Merlyn. "Amira has too."

"Are you sure?" asked Rybert.

"Yes, I am," said Merlyn. "I remember what the temple felt like before, when she was there. She has definitely gone."

"Then," said Rybert, "Gabriel is wherever Amira is."

PART II
PURNIMA AND POETRY

GUM FLAT

CHAPTER 9
RUNNING BY

Have you seen the bush by moonlight, from the train, go running by?

Blackened log and stump and sapling, ghostly trees all dead and dry;

Here a patch of glassy water; there a glimpse of mystic sky?

Have you heard the still voice calling—yet so warm, and yet so cold:

"I'm the Mother-Bush that bore you! Come to me when you are old"?

Did you see the Bush below you sweeping darkly to the Range,

All unchanged and all unchanging, yet so very old and strange!

While you thought in softened anger of the things that did estrange?

(Did you hear the Bush a-calling, when your heart was young and bold:

"I'm the Mother-Bush that nursed you; come to me when you are old"?)

In the cutting or the tunnel, out of sight of stock or shed,

Did you hear the grey Bush calling from the pine-ridge overhead:

"You have seen the seas and cities—all is cold to you, or dead—

All seems done and all seems told, but the grey-light turns to gold!

I'm the Mother-Bush that loves you—come to me now you are old"?

— *ON THE NIGHT TRAIN BY HENRY LAWSON*

CHAPTER 10
NIGHT TRAIN

O n the way to Gum Flat:
Merlyn read the Henry Lawson poem on the wall of the night train to Gum Flat. Written in 1922, the year of Lawson's passing, it was his last poem. She looked out the dark window at the even darker bush "running by" and felt a profound sense of belonging and also a profound sense of separation.

> Have you heard the still voice calling—yet so warm, and yet so cold.
>
> — H. LAWSON

It was the same land that Lawson saw, wrote about, and loved. This land doesn't really change. It is too vast, ancient, detached, motherly.

All unchanged and all unchanging, yet so very old and strange.

— H. LAWSON

Indeed, the full moon glow gave the many dead gum trees a *ghostly* appearance. It was an unforgiving environment, even for the hardiest and most tolerant of gums.

They did have tactics before succumbing to death. In the long dry periods, they cut off supply to nominated roots and associated branches to save themselves. Eventually, the dried-out branches would crack and crash to the ground, occasionally on top of unsuspecting farmers, thus giving the gums the nickname of Widow Maker.

The "running" bush under the "mystic sky" was the land of Merlyn's childhood. She left it a long time ago. Maybe, an eternity ago.

She thought she had forgotten it and was sure it had forgotten her.

Apparently, neither was true.

By rail, Gum Flat was six hours northwest of Waldmeer —flats of dry country, real bush, "in the sticks" as the locals proudly say. After all, if you can make something out of sticks, you can make something out of anything. Country folk are good at that.

After trying to book the daytime express passenger train (which was full due to short notice), Merlyn decided on the night train. As a teenager and young adult, she had used it many times on trips back and forth to the city. It was essentially a freight train with a rickety, old passenger carriage attached at the end.

Merlyn's grandmother's house was on a hill, just outside

Gum Flat, overlooking the railway track. The train was like a clock. Twice a day, she and her grandmother (and whichever other children happened to be in the house) would wave from the verandah at the occupants of the passing train. One train was this one. It arrived in Gum Flat at dawn when "the grey-light turns to gold". The other train was the daytime express passenger train, which sped past at 2.00 in the afternoon. It never seemed to occur to anyone that the strangers on the train may not look or, even if they did look, may not be interested in the folk waving to them from the farmhouse on the hill.

Once, as a child, Merlyn asked her grandmother about it.

"We don't really know them," said Merlyn seriously (she was a serious child).

"We might, Mer-Mer," said her grandmother.

"And if we don't?" asked Merlyn.

"Then we wave anyway," said her grandmother cheerily.

People in the country wave because it's important to them that they wave. The response doesn't alter what they feel they should do.

Apart from that, they don't overthink things. They have too much to do.

Merlyn did. Think, that is.

That's why she left.

That's also why she was returning to Gum Flat now.

CHAPTER 11
TIMELESS

There was a practical reason for returning to Gum Flat. Merlyn and her siblings inherited the railway station master's house after the recent death of their uncle. Due to his advanced age, he had not lived in it for years. And for years before that, it had become increasingly run-down, as happens with old people's houses. Merlyn hadn't seen her uncle in twenty years. But having no children of his own, he decided to leave the house to her and her siblings.

The decline of the western railway, which, at one time, was supreme ruler of transportation—for people, freight, and mail—seemed to break not only the spirit of the old trains but also her uncle's. That is why she hadn't seen him in so long. He didn't want to see anyone.

In his later years, he lived quietly in the nursing home of the closest town. Gum Flat didn't have a nursing home. It had a railway station, a pub, two little churches of opposing denominations, an empty police station, and several long-abandoned shops. That was it.

The night train's hypnotic trance was dissipated by the emerging gold dawn and the approaching Gum Flat station. Merlyn's thoughts were drawn back to the reality of small-town country life. *Their world is small, occasionally idyllic, but nearly always small.* She looked up at the Lawson poem.

While you thought in softened anger of the things that did estrange.

— H. LAWSON

Part of growing up involves becoming estranged from one's birth family, thought Merlyn philosophically. *If the family romance is not broken, one never truly grows up.*

Usually, we don't have to look too far to find estrangement material, but country estrangement often takes a particular form. Merlyn's father died when she was young. Uncle Ochre, a farmer, graciously took it upon himself to be the proxy father. Although the intention was commendable, it was not an easy match.

One particularly strong memory was of him asking Merlyn about her chosen career path. Like her father, he was anxious that she use her brain to get a good education in some mainstream, responsible area. However, Merlyn was already strongly inclined to other matters in life and tried to explain that she wanted to do something more spiritual.

Uncle Ochre threw his arms in the air, stormed out of the room, and said, "Religion? Religion! What sort of a job is that? Teaching Hail Marys!"

When Merlyn decided to follow her humanitarian calling as a young adult and spent much of her time working voluntarily with the homeless of the inner city, he, not surprisingly, said, "Someone else can look after them. You are wasting your life and your brain. Besides, charity begins at home. If you want to help someone, help your family."

A regular proclamation from Uncle Ochre to Merlyn was, "Common sense, Mer. Common sense! Your father. Your father!"

That was meant to mean that Merlyn did not have common sense, that her father did, and that it was Uncle Ochre's responsibility to make sure she got some common sense into her head.

It was true that common sense wasn't Merlyn's forte. She wasn't silly or stupid, but she heard so many more voices than the common-sense voice. That complicates matters. And sometimes, the other voices were much more interesting and pressing than the common common-sense voice.

Besides, for all the talk about country common sense, Merlyn thought common sense was not always sensical, and there were often more intelligent (albeit less obvious) solutions. Further, it seemed to her that what was good common sense in one environment was far from common or sensical in another environment. It was situational. City slickers can be dangerous to themselves and others in the outback, but the reverse is also true.

With the significant mismatch of worldviews, the one thing that saved the situation (long-term, if not at the time) was that Uncle Ochre viewed Merlyn as a daughter. He would have had the same response to his own daughter. Somehow, that made it bearable. Not stayable, but bearable.

As the night train whistled into the growing light of early morning and into Gum Flat station, Merlyn took one final look at the poem on the rattling train wall.

I'm the Mother-Bush that loves you—come to me now you
are old.

— H. LAWSON

I'm not old, she thought, *but somehow the bush makes everything old—maybe, timeless.*

SAME SONG SUNG

CHAPTER 12
DRUNKS AND BOGANS

In the city, at the State Ballet:

Merlyn was the last to leave the room after her weekly adult dance class at the State Ballet. She was in a quiet corner, stretching and processing her recent visit to Gum Flat.

"What's the matter with him, mouthing off like an idiot?" said a teacher entering the room with a co-worker.

Clearly, they hadn't noticed Merlyn. She was about to make her presence known, but decided to shrink further into the shadows as they continued their conversation.

"He never used to be like that," complained the teacher. "I remember when he was the golden boy—nice to everyone, caused no trouble. Not saying that he should be like that now. I mean, he's a grown-up and one of our head people. He can't be a wimp, but he is acting like a..."

"It's the piss," interrupted the other teacher.

"He's not an alcoholic," laughed the first teacher.

"You don't understand alcohol dependence," said the other. "You don't have to be lying in a hospital bed to be an alcoholic. Many alcoholics function at a high level and appear fine. But, bit by bit, as the dependence gets more control, their life starts to unravel—their body, relationships, work, ability to be productive, mood, self-respect, and will to live. I know because it runs in my family. His family, too."

He kicked aside a dust ball on the floor and continued, "For that reason, I don't drink myself. I did when I was younger, but I could smell its joy in having me join the crew. So, I gave it the flick. There isn't any other way for people who have that gene. Give it the flick, or it's gotcha. You learn that at Alcoholics Anonymous. Ben needs to learn it too."

Merlyn's heart sank.

She had told herself that they were talking about someone she didn't know, someone she didn't love, but she knew it was Ben all along.

When she lived with him, he drank every evening.

Just a wine to help me relax from the day, he would say.

It was nearly always more than one. More than two. And on weekends, more again.

He sometimes commented that there was a line in his family made up of *drunks and bogans.* He said it with such disgust. Ben was not and never would be a bogan. But a drunk? Apparently, so.

Sometimes, he would say (like all alcoholics) that it is okay if someone is a happy drunk.

There are no happy drunks. They all end up a misery.

So do the people around them.

"Can't someone tell him?" said the first teacher, whose attitude had changed from anger to concern.

"Who?" said the other. "He was married for a few years to someone called Merlyn. That didn't work out, and she's gone. Not sure where."

I'm right here, thought Merlyn with a fleeting smile in a deadly serious conversation.

"Then he hooked up with some shrink-chick, but that didn't work out either," continued the other teacher.

"If she was a psychologist, she should have been able to sort him out," said the first teacher.

"She did call him out about it," said the other. "He ended the relationship."

CHAPTER 13
SNAKE PIT

O n the way out of the building, Merlyn passed her least favourite person in the State Ballet. It was the event organiser. A woman about fifty who, with a lot of work and money, looked forty with her long, blonde hair and short, tight skirts. She was a highly manipulative person, full of smiles and full of venom.

Unfortunately, she had taken the opportunity to pair up with Ben, not as a partner but as a social ally. In return for her protection, money, and social organisation, she was seen and photographed with one of the State Ballet's most prestigious people.

She was anything but prestigious. Although a drinker (and probably drug taker) herself, she wasn't dependent on it. It wasn't in her genes, and she was too calculating. She was an ugly person, and the partnership with Ben was equally ugly. It was the sort of dysfunctional decision that an alcohol-oriented person makes.

The woman knew of Ben's past relationship with Merlyn and mostly acted as if Merlyn didn't exist. However, on other occasions, the woman would look straight at her, laugh, and whisper something to those around her. She proudly credited her nastiness to "savage confidence". Savage? Yes. Confident? Some of the most destructive things in the world are done with utter confidence.

As Merlyn walked out the double glass doors of the building and headed for the safety of Tom's cafe next door, a verse started singing its therapeutic song into her mind.

Snake pit,
snake pit.
Beware,
beware.

Snake pit,
snake pit.
Be
aware.

Happy faces,
snake pit smile.
Luscious bodies,
snake pit guile.

Lashes and teeth,
long blonde hair,
leather and lace,
snake pit lair.

Smell of booze,
snake pit breath.
Livers ageing,
snake pit death.

It's in the blood,
alcohol stung.
In the bloodline,
same song sung.

Event organiser
organisers the pit.
Snakiest of all,
in her daughter's outfit.

"Unconditional love" is
bandied about, but
the conditions are a lot
and the love is not.

CHAPTER 14
THIRD EYE

N*ext door, at Tom & Hardy:*

"Hello, my love," said Tom. "How was Gum Flat?"

"I'm back," said Merlyn.

Tom looked at Merlyn as if to say, *That's obvious, but how was it?*

"Uncle Ochre hasn't changed," said Merlyn with a finality that let Tom know she didn't wish to discuss it further.

"I'll get your coffee," said Tom.

When he returned, Merlyn smiled and said, "I'm in a performance!"

"Really?" said Tom, looking impressed. "With the State Ballet?"

"Don't be silly," said Merlyn. "As if. With the Manipura Dancers at Ajna Temple.

"Oh," said Tom, clearly unimpressed. "That's a performance, is it?"

Merlyn whacked his arm and said, "Yes, Tom."

LAST DANCE CLASS at the Waldmeer Warriors, Shambhavi announced to his devoted class of women that they would all join the Manipura Dancers in a special performance next full moon. He said he wanted them to experience first-hand the joy of sharing dance with others.

"I don't care about your technical level or fitness," said Shambhavi. "Of course, I would like it to be as good as possible, and we are going to keep working on that, but mostly I want you to know what it is like to take the dance inside you and present it in a way that other people can see and appreciate."

With his perfect body, perfect training, and perfect career, Shambhavi could have been forgiven for being disinterested in the motley lot of country dancers of all ages and abilities that faced him every week in Waldmeer. Yet, there was none of that in him. That is why the women (without exception) said yes to his project, although it would have frightened the life out of most of them. The one thing that inspires fearless devotion in followers is devotion from their leader.

"We have a lot of work to do over the next few weeks," said Shambhavi, clapping his hands together and demanding absolute attention. "Face the mirror. We will run through our little choreography. However, I want you to see your image with your *third eye*. Look at your body and imagine what your third eye can see, as an outsider, an onlooker, observing from the balcony. Detach yourself from your body and imagine it as someone else's."

That's not exactly the right use of the term "third eye", thought Merlyn. *The third eye is one's intuition, an entirely different way of seeing from the physical way. It doesn't even see bodies. It's not an additional eye, placed somewhere else, that can see things that your other two physical eyes can't see. But, hey, what does it matter? He can use the term any way he wants. Maybe that's why Shambhavi is such a good dancer. He takes things and makes them his own.*

BACK TO TOM & *Hardy today:*

"The teacher told us to look at our body as if it were someone else's," said Merlyn, "to feel that we were in someone else's body, not our own."

"I like feeling that I'm in someone else's body," said Tom.

STILL POINT

CHAPTER 15
MR PEEN'S FIRE

N *ext Purnima morning, in the city:*
The Manipura Dancers/Waldmeer Warriors collaboration was postponed, so Merlyn went to the city for the State Ballet adult class.

The State Ballet didn't normally bother with training nonprofessional adult dancers. They were far too busy with their up-and-coming talent and maintaining the professional company. However, Merlyn's class was a special promotional offer.

It was taken by a mixture of instructors. Some were probably last-minute throw-ins. She could imagine the timetable coordinator yelling in the staffroom, "Who is taking them today? Someone has to. So-and-so, it's your turn."

Merlyn didn't mind. It was a privilege to have access to the company's teachers. They were either marvellous, young, current dancers or older professionals with a great deal of experience. Whoever they were, she approached the class with the clear thought that she would get as much as possible from it.

One of the rather quaint, old-fashioned things that the company did was to call all its teachers by Mr, Mrs, or Miss. The younger ones were Mr or Miss, and their first name. The older ones were Mr, Miss, or Mrs, and their surname. Today's class was with a senior teacher, Mr Peen. He was a commanding person with an excellent dancing background.

At fifty, Mr Peen was still a captivating and energetic dancer. Sometimes, he had short appearances in the ballet, which was unusual at that age. Unlike many of the men in the company, he was not gay. He had a strong masculine demeanour, not that that was any indication of sexual preference. There were gay men in the company who also had a strong masculine energy field. They were the ones that the female dancers tended to fall in love with. They had all the attractiveness of conventional male qualities combined with the non-neediness and lack of predatory behaviour that a sexually incompatible person has towards women.

Mr Peen had a few children (spread out in age) to a few women (spread out in time). He had lived and loved. He had won and lost. He knew what he was doing. And he didn't. No one could accuse him of not trying. He was still trying. A decent, driven, principled man with a lot of fire for life. Sometimes, a little too much fire.

At Prana Community, Merlyn learned that the human body has five base elements in differing proportions: 72% water, 12% earth, 6% air, 6% ether, and 4% fire.

Whenever she looked at Mr Peen, she felt that instead of 4% fire, he got 5 or 6% fire. That might not seem much of a difference, but fire is the most potent element. Even a tiny amount brings lots of power and focus to the individual's system. Too much fire and the person will start burning up, either in the physical body or in their more subtle bodies.

Merlyn wanted to reach out and touch Mr Peen's hand so that some of the water element (which was strong in her) would flow into him as a balance.

Touching wasn't something that Merlyn generally sought. She didn't need it herself, and it didn't seem necessarily helpful to other people, although most crave it. She touched little children because they genuinely need it to grow and thrive. She touched lovers because lovers are like children in their openness, vulnerability, and playfulness. She touched people in dancing because dancers can only talk through their bodies. They have no other language.

The adult ballet class was big today, and moved along briskly. There was no time for Mr Peen to touch anyone except for the occasional quick correction. As Merlyn couldn't physically reach out and touch Mr Peen, she turned her mind to it instead. She imagined the water element moving towards him.

At that point, Mr Peen abruptly stopped talking, turned around, and looked directly at her. She was fairly sure that he didn't know why he stopped talking, turned around, or stared at her. Nevertheless, she immediately stopped doing what she was doing and remembered one of Guru Gadubanud's most uncompromising rules.

At no time are you to interfere with anyone else's energetic system without it being expressly requested or, in some manner, clearly indicated that it is their wish for you to do so.

— GURU GADUBANUD

If the guru caught people doing it (and if you were doing

it, he would catch you), he would ask you to leave the satsang and possibly the community with the words, "We are not the occult. We are a spiritual path."

Having returned to his train of thought, Mr Peen was on a roll with the phenomena of *the still point.* He explained how advanced martial artists use the still point to achieve extraordinary levels of activity, strength, and precision. He said that the mark of an accomplished dancer was the ability to dance from the still point.

Merlyn remembered hearing a poem by T. S. Eliot about the still point. It was a rare recording of the poet in 1935.

> At the still point of the turning world. Neither flesh nor fleshless;
>
> Neither from nor towards; at the still point, there the dance is,
>
> But neither arrest nor movement. And do not call it fixity,
>
> Where past and future are gathered. Neither movement from nor towards,
>
> Neither ascent nor decline. Except for the point, the still point,
>
> There would be no dance, and there is only the dance.
>
> — T. S. ELIOT

At the end of the class, Mr Peen said, "When you can be still and still dance, you are a great dancer. When you can move and still be still, you are a greater dancer."

CHAPTER 16
PURNIMA TO PURNIMA

At Tom & Hardy, that afternoon:

"Listen to this," Merlyn said to Tom after her ballet class. "At the still point of the turning world. Neither flesh nor fleshless. Neither from nor towards. At the still point, there the dance is...."

"That's nice," interrupted Tom. "But I have to work."

He returned to Merlyn when he felt he could do so without getting another poetry recital.

"I have a problem," said Merlyn.

Tom looked at her as if to say, *I know,* but decided to say, "What is it?"

"I have to be out of my flat for a while," said Merlyn. "That was the arrangement when I took it. It had a long-standing booking."

"When?" asked Tom.

"Tonight," said Merlyn. "Full moon."

Tom wasn't sure what the full moon had to do with it or anything.

"Can you stay with someone in Waldmeer?" he asked.

"I have some offers," said Merlyn. "But I don't like being around most people—to live with, I mean. Can I stay with you at the weekends? I'll go to Malik's house during the week when I have to work."

"My sofa bed is very uncomfortable," said Tom, a little too quickly. "It has a rod down the middle. I keep thinking I should buy a new one, but you know...."

Merlyn did know. He didn't want to make it comfortable, or people might come.

"I'm little," said Merlyn. "I'll lie next to the rod."

"For how long?" said Tom.

"Purnima to Purnima," said Merlyn.

"Purnima to Purnima?" repeated Tom.

"One month," said Merlyn.

"Okay, you can stay on the weekends," said Tom. "I'll be at work anyway, but don't go doin' my head in. Keep your Purnimas to yourself."

CHAPTER 17
THERE THE DANCE IS

*A*t Tom's apartment, that evening:

As Merlyn tossed and turned on Tom's uncomfortable sofa bed that evening, she could see the full moon peeping through the balcony curtains. She got up (yet again), made some herbal tea, walked around, drew back the curtains, and stared at the night sky. Her thoughts were broken by Tom opening his bedroom door.

"Sorry," said Merlyn. "Am I waking you up?"

Tom rolled his eyes as if to say, *Of course you are. You are rummaging around like some nocturnal creature.*

Merlyn looked at the sofa bed by way of explanation, but, as beggars can't be choosers, she didn't want to say anything. Tom gestured with resignation for her to sleep on the other side of his bed. He pointedly placed little Hardy in the middle of them and went back to sleep without a single word.

It's a good body, thought Merlyn as she looked at Tom's sleeping body. *Very aligned.*

A lot of sexual desire comes from believing that another

body can alleviate our aloneness. It can't do that, but people think it can, and when one body doesn't work, they look for another. Merlyn didn't feel alone, so she didn't look for anyone's body or personality to fill the void. Nevertheless, unlike Tom (who was not interested in her body as a woman), Merlyn's programming was for the body that Tom had.

I better stop thinking about this, thought Merlyn, *because if Tom is anything like me and picks up on other people's thoughts, he will kick me out of his bed and house.*

Tom was sleeping so motionlessly that Merlyn, once again, remembered the still-point poem,

At the still point of the turning world. Neither flesh nor fleshless;

Neither from nor towards; at the still point, there the dance is.

— T. S. ELIOT

She closed her eyes and fell into a deep, still sleep.

TWENTY MILE TRACK

CHAPTER 18
PUDDLE MUDDLE

In Waldmeer at Twenty Mile Track:

It was midweek and midwinter, so there were not many tourists in Waldmeer. On this early morning, Twenty Mile Track was deserted.

The track started on the beach at Waldmeer Boathouse Cafe, continued over the swing bridge, and followed the river into the forested Lelek hills. The river quickly thinned its waistline into a more manageable, bubbling, green-flanked waterway.

The Purnima Passage clearing was at an early point of the track. There was no huge ball of light there today. It only lit up once a month. And only, Merlyn assumed, for those who had eyes to see. Whenever Merlyn passed through the clearing to walk further along the track, she could sense its simmering power. Laying low but definitely not absent.

Every step further into the Leleks created a more meditative, receptive state of mind. The chattering water and moving greenness had a lulling effect on one's consciousness. Trekking rhythmically along through the puddles,

Merlyn started singing a little song, in her mind, about the calming effect of the forest track.

> Puddle, puddle,
> muddled muddle.
>
> Muddled mind,
> entangled tangle.
>
> Puddle, puddle,
> unmuddle the muddle.
>
> Still mind,
> untangle the tangle.
>
> Puddle, puddle,
> mind the mind.
>
> Still mind.
> Mind. Still.

CHAPTER 19
LINES AND LOONIES

After a while, Merlyn started to sing her *Puddle Muddle* song aloud. She then thought about the difference between talking to oneself in one's mind and talking to oneself out loud. If you listen to someone talking to themselves, they are basically saying the same thing that people say to themselves in their minds. The difference is generally not in the content, but that they are saying it out loud. The demarcation of sanity is the line between talking silently to oneself and talking those same thoughts out loud, in public, unchecked and unawares.

If one wants to venture into extra-sensory experiences of life, then one should have a firm grip on that line. Otherwise, the fine line of sanity will be transgressed, and the person may have a hard time retrieving it, which explains why many "spiritual" groups are full of loonies.

As Merlyn sang to the trees, they seemed to reach down and join in. The wind picked up, and the water jumped joyously over the river rocks. The birds listened and then sang back their version. The puddles squelched, happy to be gainfully employed. The waning moon peeked through the trees. The sun, although up, was not high enough to completely dominate the sky. The moon still had some glow as it edged towards the western horizon.

CHAPTER 20
MONTHLY CYCLE

Merlyn recalled one of Guru Gadubanud's comments that no matter where it was in its monthly cycle, the moon always has its face turned towards Earth. He said that the day it started to look away from us would be the beginning of our decline as we currently know it.

The moon always has its face to us, thought Merlyn, *because that is part of its geometrically perfect tracking path around Earth. That, in turn, affects the Earth's geometrically perfect tracking path around the sun. If the moon's orbit was even slightly altered (by the endless possibility of things that can and probably do happen in the universe), then our planet would also change its orbit around the sun. The Earth's population would adjust to the changes and stop reproducing. Eventually, humans would cease to exist. Other life forms would probably remain longer as many are more malleable than us.*

These thoughts weren't in the slightest distressing to Merlyn. On the contrary, she thought it was a rather gentle and kind way for humanity to eventually decline. Besides, if we can appear on a brilliant blue gem of a planet at some point in time and space, we can reappear elsewhere. Creation doesn't stop. It changes. It's the changes that help it to continue on its constant creative path.

On hearing a breaking branch, Merlyn abruptly turned around. She wondered if someone was nearby. Being alone in the woods can be disconcerting as a female. However, she put her mind to rest with the thought, *If by chance, I stumble across someone, the likelihood of them being crazy is negligible. I'm the only crazy person out here!*

PART III
STONES OF SPRING

AUGUST ASHES

CHAPTER 21
THE GIANT SCHOOL STALKER

I n *Waldmeer:*
The month of Merlyn's weekend sleepovers at Tom's flat and weekday sleepovers at Malik's house was at an end. Neither was ideal. Tom kept pushing her away. And Malik's large, noisy household was all-consuming, with three children (Maria, the youngest at fourteen, and Michael, the oldest at twenty), two adults (Malik and Rachael), and Odin, who was supposed to be an adult but on Earth ended up more of a dependent.

It may not have been Merlyn's favourite arrangement, but that's life, isn't it? When are things perfectly balanced on the outside? Rarely. And in those glorious moments when they are, it doesn't last long. The only viable option is to try and balance ourselves on the inside so that we are not pushed around by what happens outside us.

On Merlyn's final evening at Malik's, before returning to her flat across the road, there was a heated but hushed conversation about Odin.

"Someone has to take him back to Borderfirma," said

Rachael, who had recovered from the illness that precipitated Merlyn working in the Waldmeer Warriors. "He has been here since the end of summer, which is six months. Odin doesn't belong in Waldmeer—or anywhere on Earth."

Like the rest of the family, Rachael loved Odin. How could you not love someone who was utterly devoted to your well-being? And therein lay the problem. Odin didn't have enough to do, so he invented jobs.

"He is a little politically incorrect," said Malik reluctantly (Odin was his link to the Borderfirma Mountains and his mother).

"He is not only politically incorrect," said Rachael. "He is *everything* incorrect. You know what he's like in the gym. He treats everyone as if they are his incompetent students of the Great Valley and sends them off to scale trees and drag lumps of wood. People find him odd. He tells our gentler male clients to *man up,* our overweight ones that they are *fat slobs,* and our skinny ones to *grow some balls.* It's unacceptable."

Malik couldn't help laughing. Although he understood Odin's training style (as Odin had trained him), it was hardly Earth-appropriate. Rachael didn't laugh.

"And you know what he's like with Maria," she said. "He can't accept that she is growing up. He stands at the school fence during the day like a giant stalker, waiting for her to come out at recess and lunch. Then he watches her like a hawk to make sure no one is mean to her. Maria doesn't say anything because she's Maria, but it makes her life difficult."

At the mention of his dear heart child, Maria, Malik sighed and said to his wife, "Your health has greatly improved."

Turning to Merlyn, he said, "Rachael can return to work

now. So, why don't you go to Borderfirma with Odin for a month? Purnima Passage will be open tomorrow night. You can tell Odin that you need an escort while you are there. Hopefully, he will resettle in Borderfirma, and you can return home alone."

"Do you think he will adjust after your mother's passing?" asked Merlyn.

She hesitated to bring up Faith-Amira's death, but it seemed best to talk about it. Amira's sudden and unexpected death was the reason for Gabriel's abrupt return to Earth, along with the travelling trio of Odin, Maria, and Rybert.

"Mum would want us to focus on the day's gains, not the losses," said Malik.

"No one tell Maria," said Rachael. "Or she will be back there in a wink. I can't go through that again, not knowing when and if she will be home."

Malik didn't need convincing on that issue. The plan to get *the giant school stalker* back to his rightful home would not be repeated from his lips.

CHAPTER 22
TEMPLE THIEF

The next afternoon, in Prana Community:

T On the threshold of spring, the late August afternoon was cold but sunny. Merlyn was preparing for Purnima Passage. However, she decided to make a quick visit to Ajna Temple. It had been two months since Gabriel's body had been found there, and Amira's spirit had disappeared. Merlyn hadn't been back since then. She thought that the temple would somehow seem empty. That's what happens when you get used to the world of spirits. If they aren't around, it's a bit boring.

Next to the black granite linga, a marked tin ceremoniously sat in the place where Gabriel's body had been discovered. It was his ashes. Due to the police enquiry, his body had only recently been returned to Prana Community. He was cremated. The ashes were to stay beside the linga until full moon, when they would be dispersed over the sea.

That will be tonight, thought Merlyn, *after the Manipura Dancers perform.*

Shambhavi's Waldmeer Warrior's dance class hadn't had

their opportunity to join the Manipura Dancers because he said he was waiting for the right full moon. None of the women knew what would make it *right,* but they trustingly left that to him. Through the stained-glass window, Merlyn saw the sun slanting towards the western horizon and thought, *I better go.*

"It's not only Odin who doesn't belong here. It's you, too," she suddenly said as she grabbed the tin of ashes.

Stuffing the tin under her coat, she ran to her car. It wasn't the calmest approach for a thief, but Merlyn was a poor criminal.

CHAPTER 23
DUOS AND TRIOS

That evening, at Twenty Mile Track:

"We're now the *travelling duo* instead of the *travelling trio*," said Odin chirpily as he stood at the entrance of Purnima Passage.

"We are still a trio," said Merlyn, pulling the tin of ashes from under her coat.

Odin frowned and said, "I know why we are returning to Borderfirma."

"You do?" said Merlyn.

"Yes," said Odin. "I've done a lot of thinking since I've been in Waldmeer. It's the first time I have had so much time to myself. In the beginning, I hated it. All I could think about was Lady Faith."

He gazed at the pulsing, round ball of light before him. It had become brighter since they had stood there.

"Not by choice (but by circumstance), I went through a lot of things in my mind," said Odin. "I'm not too proud to say that I often cried. But, after a while, I realised that something was doing me good. The deaths of Lady Faith and my mother didn't seem as painful anymore."

Merlyn smiled at him encouragingly. Odin, of all people, was changing.

"I am ready to face my fears and continue with my life," said Odin.

Pointing to the tin, he added, "I think it would be fair to say that Borderfirma is as much Gabriel's home as mine."

A nearby owl seemed to be agreeing.

"Now that Lady Faith has gone," said Odin, "it seems silly to keep to my old ways about Gabriel. I know it was jealousy. I loved Lady Faith as much as he did. Probably more, but...."

"But what?" asked Merlyn.

"I wasn't good enough for someone like Lady Faith," said Odin.

Although Merlyn dearly wanted to reassure him that that wasn't the case, she felt it best to let life be life.

"So," continued Odin, "I settled on serving and protecting her to the best of my ability. I accepted that I wasn't good enough for her, but I always felt that neither was Gabriel. Yet, she chose to be with him all those years. Why? He did so many wrong things, but something in her loved him in a way she didn't love me."

He took the ashes from Merlyn's hands. She was a little concerned that they might end up being thrown into the dark territory of the owl. Odin felt her hesitation and laughed.

"I'll look after them," said Odin. "I'll do it for Lady Faith. And I'll do it for Gabriel."

With that, he made a grand gesture towards the Passage and said, "After you, Lady Merlyn."

This is going to be easier than I imagined, thought Merlyn.

STONE GROUND

CHAPTER 24
RETURN OF THE SNAKES

I n the *Borderfirma Lowlands, at Stone Ground:*
Merlyn and Odin exited Purnima Passage at Stone Ground on that August full moon. They were surprised to see red warning tape around the sacred rock structure.

"At least it still works as a portal," said Merlyn when Aristotle and Indra came out of the palace to greet them.

"It does," said Aristotle. "But for how long?"

"What happened to it?" asked Odin, who had jumped the tape and was inspecting the rock closely.

"A large crack appeared in it recently," said Indra. "It could fall on someone."

Stone Ground was a linga like the granite one in Ajna temple, and also like Floating Cave (which was a wet linga). Floating Cave and Stone Ground were ancient. Both had been used for energetic purposes for longer than Borderfirma's history had been recorded.

Like all lingas, they needed energetic upkeep. Floating Cave was in the good hands of the monk at Floating Cave

Monastery. The responsibility for the upkeep of Stone Ground fell to Aristotle and Indra.

"We can stop the rock from falling on people," said Aristotle. "That is the least of the problems. The real problem is that, since cracking, Stone Ground has been losing its spiritual balance."

"Do you know how it happened?" asked Merlyn.

"We have our suspicions," said Aristotle, turning to Indra.

"When Evanora took over the Borderfirma Lowlands," said Indra, "she used the linga for destructive purposes. After her, much effort went into repairing it so it could function beneficially again."

"Who fixed it?" asked Merlyn.

"Indra and I were only thirteen. It wasn't us," said Aristotle. "After seven years, Stone Ground had healed enough for us to move into the palace."

"Does Evanora have something to do with this?" asked Odin.

"Indra thinks so," said Aristotle.

"The pythons have returned," said Indra.

CHAPTER 25
RACK AND RUIN

L ike her father, Indra was an expert snake handler and a lover of the poisonous creatures (especially cobras, the native snake of the Lowlands).

"Before Evanora, we never had a snake problem," said Indra. "Left to themselves, snakes are gentle, intelligent creatures."

Merlyn recalled that a spiralling snake around a rod symbolises the medical profession on Earth. In the East, a coiled snake starting at the base of the spine and travelling upwards to the crown represents kundalini or life force.

"Evanora populated the Lowlands with her species of snake—Pythons," continued Indra. "They bred out of control, and in defence, the cobras did likewise. As a result, they all became vicious to each other and to people. We haven't seen any pythons for a long time, and the cobras have peacefully kept to themselves. However, the pythons have returned, and the cobras are getting snitchy."

"Is Evanora still alive?" asked Merlyn.

"Last time I was here, she was," said Odin. "After the

Borderfirma Battle, she went mad and was committed to the psychiatric hospital. She has lived there for twenty years."

"She died a few weeks after Mum died," said Aristotle. "Not long after Odin left."

Odin thought about that momentarily, stood tall, and said, "It's just as well I have returned. I can see things go to rack and ruin when I'm away."

RING OF SILVER

CHAPTER 26
GO TO THE MONASTERY

I n the *Borderfirma Lowlands, at Stone Ground:*
Over the next month, Aristotle, Indra, Odin, and Merlyn tried, rather fruitlessly, to repair the crack in Stone Ground. The more they tried, the less it cooperated. Their very trying seemed to give energy to the force which had overtaken it. These words kept repeating in Merlyn's mind whenever she was near Stone Ground. She didn't know where they came from or what they meant.

> The forces are gathering
> as we sit in this room.
> The darkness amasses
> bringing its doom.
>
> The sides are chosen,
> the wheels in motion.
> Go to the monastery,
> set your devotion.

The last useless battle,
someone will fall.
Useless, but useful.
For nothing, for All.

One day, on hearing Merlyn sing the poem, Aristotle asked, "Where did you hear those words?"

"Here, at Stone Ground," said Merlyn. "Do you know what they mean?"

"Yes," said Aristotle. "They are the words that Nina's crystal ball said to my mother before the Borderfirma Battle."

"What did your mother do then?" asked Merlyn, who was concerned that she was not up to doing whatever Faith-Amira could do.

"She went to Floating Cave Monastery for a year on her own," said Aristotle. "Then the battle came and went."

"Where did it go?" asked Merlyn.

Aristotle smiled and said, "Mum told all the soldiers to return to their homelands and asked for the best mystic of each to come to her. One of them was the monk who still lives in the monastery. He was old even back then."

"And the other mystics?" asked Merlyn.

"My sister, Bethany, who rules the Borderfirma Mountains, didn't know who her best mystic was," said Aristotle. "She told Nina to ask her crystal ball. The ball said it was me, even though I was only thirteen."

Aristotle looked away to divert attention from the grandness of that discovery. His eyes focused on Stone Ground with its precariously tilting alignment.

"The battle ended because no one fed it," said Aristotle. "Not the slightest energy went into the conflict from our end.

Evanora, of course, would have continued with or without our energy, but the people lost interest in the conflict. Without the people, Evanora was powerless. That sent her mad."

"Now that she doesn't have a body," said Merlyn, "she could be looking for another place to reside for a second attempt—Stone Ground."

"Exactly," said Aristotle.

Walking around Stone Ground, deep in thought, he quietly repeated, "The sides are chosen, the wheels in motion. Go to the monastery, set your devotion."

He then exclaimed, "Merlyn, go!"

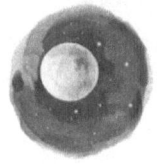

CHAPTER 27
SET YOUR DEVOTION

September full moon, at Floating Cave Monastery:

S "I can't wear it," said Merlyn. "I can't wear any jewellery. I don't like the feeling of metal on my body. It interferes with something in me—something moving out of me."

"It does, indeed," said the monk of Floating Cave Monastery. "Metal interferes with the flow of energy moving in and out of an individual, but most people don't notice it. It's subtle. The very fact that it does this is one of the reasons you must wear it. You will be immersed in deep sadhana for the next month until October Purnima. The ring will be grounding for you."

"Can't I ground in another way?" asked Merlyn.

"Although important, the grounding is the least power of this ring," said the monk. "It is consecrated in a certain way and has the collective power of all the Lowland mystics who have worked to preserve the integrity of Floating Cave and Stone Ground. You need their help."

"That's very impressive help," said Merlyn, rolling the ring between her fingers.

It was silver and shaped like a coiled snake. She tried it on the middle finger of her right hand, as it was too large for any of her other fingers.

"No," said the monk abruptly. "Take it off."

She immediately did so and felt that she was playing with a fire she didn't understand and perhaps couldn't.

"The ring must only be worn on the ring finger of the left hand," said the monk.

"The marriage finger?" queried Merlyn.

"Yes," said the monk. "It's not by accident that wedding rings are placed on the left-hand ring finger. There is a particular dedicated power in that part of the body that nearly all cultures instinctively understand. When you marry someone, it is a deep bond. Even if you divorce, they will be part of your body—your physical and etheric structures."

"If I wear the ring, then I will be married to its source," said Merlyn.

"Yes," said the monk, "there is no other way. After your month of sadhana, you will need to return to Earth. You will then be free to take the ring with you or take it off. However, I warn you. Once you experience the power and beauty of the energy that runs through this ring, you will not take it off lightly."

"You know what?" said Merlyn with a smile. "That finger has no ring. I'm on my own. Let's give it a whirl!"

The monk closed his eyes, said some words in another language, and ceremoniously placed the ring on Merlyn's left ring finger.

"One more thing," said the monk. "The ring attracts

snakes. Be careful. They are no trifling enemy and no easy friend."

THE NEXT MORNING, as Merlyn started her journey back to the Lowlands palace, she noticed that the ring had perfectly moulded itself to her finger. No longer loose. Not too tight. It fit so well that she could almost forget it was there.

PART IV
KEEP ONLY THAT

HEALING RING

CHAPTER 28
SADHANA

In the Borderfirma Lowlands, at Stone Ground:

As the monk of Floating Cave Monastery requested, Merlyn sat next to Stone Ground for most of the month doing her sadhana. She had asked the monk what type of sadhana or spiritual exercise he wanted her to do. He said there were many he could teach her, but the quickest and easiest was the way of devotion.

"How do I do devotion sadhana?" asked Merlyn.

"Don't do anything," said the monk. "Get rid of every-thing—except your love. Keep only that."

So, that is what Merlyn tried to do.

The physical posture of sitting was more manageable because of her time at Prana Community. She walked to break up the sitting, but never far from Stone Ground.

Without the silver snake ring, she did not think that her sitting would have had much impact on repairing the linga. However, with the power of all the Lowland mystics backing her, Stone Ground significantly improved. It wasn't fixed, but it was more stable.

On that note, she returned to Waldmeer on October Purnima.

She returned without Odin, but definitely not without the ring.

CHAPTER 29
WASHED AWAY WITH TEARS

Back on Earth, in the city, at the State Ballet:
A few days after her return to Waldmeer, Merlyn travelled to the city for her adult ballet class. When she arrived, no one was in the room. Eventually, Mr Peen came.

"Great," said Merlyn. "We have you today."

Mr Peen looked at her closely to try and place her.

Merlyn put out her hand and said, "I'm Merlyn. I've been to your class before. You probably don't remember me."

"Yes, I remember you," said Mr Peen. "But I'm sorry, my dear, the adult ballet class finished last month."

"Oh, did it?" asked Merlyn. "I've been away for the last two months."

"I'm here to practise," said Mr Peen. "You are welcome to use the space, too, if you like."

Mr Peen was one of the few older teachers who bothered to still dance.

"Thank you," said Merlyn. "It would be a long drive back to Waldmeer, having not done a darn thing."

For a fifty-year-old man, Mr Peen pushed himself hard. He was quite unforgiving towards his body. He didn't look at Merlyn the entire time he was practising. He was focused only on what he wanted to achieve in his practice session.

He has the mentality, thought Merlyn, *to achieve a lot. Most people do not have the mental or emotional ability to be so one-pointed in their attention. They constantly get pulled in conflicting directions because they neither understand themselves nor anything else.*

Since wearing the ring, Merlyn had become aware of many things about people that previously were somewhat muddied waters in her mind.

In his break, Mr Peen turned his dark, intent eyes towards Merlyn and said, "Thank you for not bothering me with chatter. Most people talk so much. It drives me crazy."

"Pleasure," said Merlyn with a smile. It is not every day that people thank you for not opening your mouth.

Almost as a reward for not bothering him, Mr Peen shared, "Today is the one-year anniversary of my mother's death."

"I'm sorry," said Merlyn.

"It's not my mother's death. It's my father," explained Mr Peen as he swore and wiped his wet eyes. "I don't know what has gotten into me."

Not wanting to interrupt the important healing moment, Merlyn silently touched her ring with her thumb. Mr Peen followed her movements. He would have assumed it was a wedding ring. He was old enough not to be a romantic. The romance would have been washed out of him by now by tears. In its place would be growing the love that comes with age, the love that no longer sees life as so segmented, so black and white. It knows that life and people are complicated.

"My father couldn't bear to lose my mother," said Mr Peen. "In my entire life, I never saw him cry. But when he rang to tell me about my mother, he was a broken man. Something in the sound of my Dad sobbing demolished a million castles in my mind."

Merlyn felt that Mr Peen's tears were organising the abundant fire in him into a more contained entity. *That's what healing does,* she thought. *It balances things so that **we** are more balanced.*

After a moment, Mr Peen jumped up, held out a hand, and said, "Come and have a quick dance with me before I go."

Taking his outstretched hand, Merlyn thought, *Someone can touch us and keep their energy to themselves. And someone can touch us and let their being run through their fingers into ours.*

CHAPTER 30
NO ONE CAME

At Tom & Hardy, that afternoon:

Tom was in a mood. He took one look at Merlyn's ring and rolled his eyes. He knew that she wouldn't have married anyone. His sharp mind quickly worked out that it must be a spiritual ring. He assumed it was from Prana Community, as he knew nothing about Borderfirma. He also assumed that whatever she had been doing for the last two months must have had something to do with the ring. He decided he couldn't care less and acted as if he hadn't even noticed her two-month absence.

"Have you had a good week?" he asked.

"The adult ballet class isn't on anymore," said Merlyn. "It finished while I was away."

Tom shrugged and walked off. However, he realised he hadn't taken her order and had to return, which only annoyed him further.

After eating, Merlyn felt there was not much point in staying. However, as there was no longer a Friday class, she needed to talk to Tom (mood or not) about her future visits.

"As my class is over," she said as Tom was within hearing distance, "and it's a long way to come...."

"Yes," said Tom, interrupting her. "Don't come."

Merlyn looked at Tom piercingly to try and find *her* Tom, who seemed to be doing a fine job of hiding himself.

"Don't look at me like that," said Tom. "I hate it. That's why we have bodies. To stop trespassers."

Merlyn couldn't help laughing. When Tom was mad, his psychological insight, sarcastic wit, and unintentional wisdom combined to create a humorous show.

"Come on," said Merlyn, touching his arm. "Don't be angry. I'm asking for your input."

"No, you're not," said Tom. "You're not really."

Merlyn sighed. She didn't want to waste the opportunity to help him process whatever needed processing. It could be ages before he got to that same point again.

"What I'm trying to ask is this," said Merlyn. "Is it worth my coming all this way to see you?"

"I'm gay," said Tom, implying that Merlyn was an unsolicited pursuer.

Merlyn fired up and said, "I stayed with you a whole month of weekends, sometimes in your bed. Did I ever, even once, ask you for more than friendship?"

Tom bent over the table, moved his face close to Merlyn's, and said in a slow, loaded way, "I don't want to be friends."

"You don't have to love me," said Merlyn as she stood up. "Just love somebody. Anybody. The next person who walks in the door."

As Merlyn headed for the exit, she spotted one of the Thomas Hardy quotes on the bathroom wall.

But no one came. Because no one ever does.

— *T. HARDY*

She was staring at it and ran into one of the ballet teachers from next door.

"Sorry, Benedict," she said. She knew him by name and nature.

"It's fine, love," said Benedict because he was a sweetheart.

FLAME

CHAPTER 31
MADE TO BE USED

I n the city, outside *Tom & Hardy:*
Benedict was not the only person Merlyn encountered when leaving Tom & Hardy. Ben and Esther were leaving the State Ballet at the same time. On seeing Merlyn, Esther turned away. Ben glanced at Merlyn's ringed finger, looked shocked, and quickly walked towards his car.

A FEW DAYS LATER, at *Waldmeer Warriors:*
"My city ballet class has finished," Merlyn said to Shambhavi before the Waldmeer Warrior's dance class. "So, you are my only dance guru now."

Shambhavi winked and said, "Good. I'm the only flame. That's the way I like it."

Instead of immediately starting with the dance program, Shambhavi told the class, "Ladies, I have a confession to make."

Once a Catholic, always a Catholic, thought Merlyn.

Everyone listened attentively but unbelievingly to their teacher's need for confession.

"Many months ago, I told you we would perform at Ajna Temple with the Manipura Dancers," said Shambhavi. "Then, I told you I was waiting for the right full moon. I sat in the temple a few days ago and asked myself what I was waiting for."

"You are probably waiting for us to get better," one of the women said apologetically.

Shambhavi approached her and said, "No, it is not that. You have done everything I have asked. I love and admire all of you."

There was a collective "Aww."

"The problem is not you," said Shambhavi. "And it's not the moon. It's me."

"Nonsense," said one of the women.

Shambhavi laughed, saying, "November full moon is only a few weeks away. The flame needs to burn bright for our coming Purnima."

The idea of burning reminded Shambhavi of his favourite poem, which he recited to Merlyn close to a year ago in Ajna Temple. At that time, she was having trouble with the program of asanas, kriyas, bandhas, and meditation. The meditation part was natural for her. The rest was not. It was hard work. It was meant to be. Guru Gadubanud would say you're not working hard enough if the body was not complaining. He didn't just mean for yogis. He meant for everyone because that is how the body is constructed. It is made to be used. The more, the better. Shambhavi explained to Merlyn that he had applied his dancing knowledge to the yoga tradition, which made all the difference.

Today, Shambhavi recited his poem again to the class.

Dancing is my yoga.
I do it every day.
Ancient as the Eastern one;
highway and gateway.

Proper posture.
Straight spine.
Lit up, heated up.
Fire is mine.

Free-flow energy.
Life-force flow.
Open the channels,
activate the glow.

When I'm walking,
I'm rumba-ing along.
Running for the bus,
cha-cha-ing like a song.

Pay attention
or left will trip up right.
Pay attention
or partner will fight.

Spine up.
Step up.
Close up.
Burn up.

CHAPTER 32
FEED AND BURN

After the class, Shambhavi pointed to Merlyn's left hand and asked, "Are you back with Ben?"

The two men knew each other. They came from different dancing backgrounds but had crossed paths many times over the years. Ben knew Shambhavi as Renato, which was his birth name.

"No," said Merlyn, "not at all. I saw Ben last Friday with Esther. She must have returned from Guru Gadubanud's ashram."

"Yes," said Shambhavi. "I've also seen her. To be honest...."

It always amused Merlyn when Shambhavi said, "To be honest." He didn't realise it was a way of saying, "I'm not normally honest, but..." However, the normal channels of societal communication are generally not honest or authentic.

"She has been in India for eight months," continued Shambhavi, "but I'm not sure how much it has helped her.

She seems more spiritual on the outside, but on the inside? I'm not convinced."

Shambhavi returned his eyes to Merlyn's ring and looked at her enquiringly. She wished she could tell him about Borderfirma, but that would not be a favour to anyone.

"It's a spiritual ring," said Merlyn. "It reminds me of being married to the Divine."

Shambhavi understood because that's why he changed his name to the yogic one. It symbolised rebirth as an adult fully committing to the spiritual path.

"I'm not sure I can keep wearing my ring," said Merlyn. "People keep noticing it and think I have a mysterious husband hiding somewhere. If I tell them it's a spiritual ring, they warn me to be very careful about gurus because they only want your money or sex or both."

Shambhavi laughed. The thought of his guru wanting either was absurd.

Thinking about Shambhavi's "confession" in the class, Merlyn ventured, "Do you feel you need a change?"

"Me?" said Shambhavi. "No, I have a great life! I have everything a man could want. Gorgeous wife, wonderful community, fantastic career. What more could a man want?"

Indeed, thought Merlyn, *what more could a man want? More than wife, community, and career? There is a life beyond. Much more, much less. There is a flame that both feeds you and burns you up.*

REBORN

CHAPTER 33
OLD-NEW

November full moon, at Ajna Temple:

Before the Manipura Dancers and Waldmeer Warrior Dancers started their performance, Shambhavi spoke about why their dancing took such an earthy, sensual form.

"It may seem odd to some of you," said Shambhavi to the audience, "that the Manipura Dancers deliberately (and almost exclusively) focus on the lower chakras of the body. All the odder perhaps because we are dancing in the pure and unique setting of Ajna Temple. The three energy centres we concentrate on are: Muladhara (at the base of the spine), Svadhisthana (at the pelvis), and Manipura (at the navel)."

He paused for a moment and then said, "Together, these centres control the health and balance of our basic physical needs—food, sleep, and sex. They control our ability to be creative. They give us emotional stability and enough personal power to achieve what we want. They may be chakras that align with the lower elements of life, but without them, all our work in the more spiritual and intuitive centres would be fraught with difficulties. Guru Gadubanud forbids his students from going too deeply into their sadhana without strong and stable lower chakras. So, please, do not think that we dancers are just mucking around, having fun, and not doing much of any use. We are building the foundational structure so that all the higher energies will find a suitable home in us."

Ide, a long-time member of the Waldmeer Warrior's Dancers, looked approvingly at Merlyn. They were both happily surprised by the depth of understanding that Shambhavi had recently acquired.

CHAPTER 34
BLESSED

After the performance, Shambhavi spoke again.

"This will be the last performance of the Manipura Dancers. I have decided to move back to the city. I have been offered some excellent dancing work there. Ten years ago, when I first came to Prana Community because of Veronica, I couldn't have been happier. I found a spiritual path I genuinely connected with and a community where I felt at home. Early on, I was able to form the Manipura Dancers and was given my name (which means *something born from happiness*). They said that when I dance, something blissful comes alive."

Shambhavi looked towards the window and said, "Life is not a straight-line course. What was once perfect for us may no longer be. I am not the same person I was when I came here. None of us is. I will be returning to my birth name, Renato. My birth name means to be reborn. I was born once and given that name. I was born a second time here in Prana Community and took on a new name. Now, I will be born a third time with an old-new name. I can't say *third-time lucky* because I have been lucky my whole life. I could say *third-time blessed.*"

At the end of the evening, when everyone was leaving, Renato pointed to a small, round hole in the temple wall and asked Merlyn, "Do you know what this hole is for?"

"No," said Merlyn. "I have noticed it before, but thought it needed repair."

"Look through it," said Renato.

Merlyn saw a landmass jutting out into the sea along the distant coastline.

"It's Waldmeer!" she said.

"Yes," said Renato. "Some say that it is because of Ajna Temple that Waldmeer is such a blessed place."

WHAT WE MUST KEEP

CHAPTER 35
DARK AND DEEP

*A*t *Twenty Mile Track:*

On the way home from Ajna Temple, Merlyn suddenly knew what to do about Stone Ground.

She parked at the entrance to Twenty Mile Track. The full moon didn't have a chance with thick cloud cover and the tree canopy acting as a second light blocker.

It was dark. In the country, it can be so dark that you can't even see your hand.

She slowly picked her way along the rocky track and was careful to avoid the mossy rocks next to the riverbank. Eventually, she spotted the glow of Purnima Passage.

In the Borderfirma Lowlands:

The palace grounds were deserted. It was late at night, and no one knew Merlyn was coming. She found her familiar spot next to Stone Ground and settled into a deep meditation. The monk's words became her mantra.

Get rid of everything—except your love.
Get rid of everything—except your love.
Keep only that.
Keep only that.
Keep only that.

Deep, deep, deeper into the centre of Stone Ground, the centre of herself, the centre of creation, the centre of devotion, the centre of love.

I thought that the most important love was for the Divine, thought Merlyn. *It's not. The Divine is inevitable, inescapable. It doesn't need love. It is love—in all its tiny, grand, whispering, explosive, destructive, birthing ways. The most important love is for people. They are what we must keep.*

CHAPTER 36
SUNRISE

As Merlyn went deeper into her meditation, she lost sight of the bonds tying her to Earth and Borderfirma. She merged with the past, present, and future forces of Stone Ground, Floating Cave, and all the mystics who fed the Lowland's energetic systems. Time became meaningless. Space both collapsed and expanded. Matter merged in one unbroken flow of luminosity.

"Come back. Come back," said a voice. "You are going too far away."

The voice was like a rope. It wound itself around Merlyn's mind and pulled her up, up, up into the daylight. She opened her eyes. It was first light. Thin beams of crystal white bounced off Stone Ground and continued into the early morning freshness. Odin was peering at her.

"I've been here all night," said Odin. "The monk told me to come."

Merlyn stood unsteadily, leaned on the rock, and ran her hand down its smooth surface.

"Look," said Merlyn. "The crack in Stone Ground has almost completely joined."

"Where is your ring?" asked Odin.

"In the rock," said Merlyn.

"The snakes were here last night," said Odin uncomfortably.

He had a fear of snakes. He never talked about it, but everyone knew. Merlyn was used to the cobras sitting near her during her month of sadhana beside the rock. At first, they frightened her. With time, she realised that they meant no harm. On the contrary, they meant good. Most of the time, they looked like they were just casually lying in the sun, but if the occasional python appeared, the cobras made a protective wall between her and the intruding python.

"Which ones were here?" asked Merlyn.

"Both," said Odin nervously.

Merlyn smiled. Knowing Odin's fear of them, he was brave to keep watch over her. He shuddered at the memory of them, and an object fell from his pocket. It was Gabriel's ashes.

"I thought you put Gabriel's ashes to rest in the Great Valley three months ago," said Merlyn.

"I was going to," said Odin, "but something stopped me every time I went to do it. I didn't know if it was him wanting to stay or me not wanting to throw him back to the soil."

"It's not good to keep him here," said Merlyn. "Gabriel is not evolved enough to consciously choose where his spirit will go after death. The dead can cling to where they came from for too long if they don't know what else to do or if someone is willing them to be here. He needs to be put to rest properly so that his journey will continue the right way."

At that moment, one of the cobras slid halfway up Stone

Ground. Odin jumped. The tin of ashes went flying, hit the rock, lost its lid, and Gabriel's ashy body fell into the remaining crack of Stone Ground. The sun reached the horizon and sent a yellow beam of light onto the rock. Stone Ground completely closed, with Gabriel's ashes inside.

"Is that alright?" asked Odin, concerned that he may have inadvertently sent Gabriel to the wrong place.

Merlyn placed her hand on the rock and said, "Yes, it's alright. His life force has contributed to the healing of Stone Ground. The ring will direct him out and on his way to the Homeland where he belongs."

PERFECT PURNIMA

CHAPTER 37
BEST INTEREST

N *ovember Purnima, on Earth:*
When Stone Ground was healed, certain other things were impacted in a healing way. The moment the rising sun hit the horizon in the Borderfirma Lowlands and closed the rock, a burst of energy shot out into Borderfirma and Earth. As it was such a powerful force, it changed those it reached in some significant way.

At that moment, Ben was sleeping. Most dancers are not early risers. They often work in the evening, so their dinner and sleep cycles tend to be late. In his unconsciousness, he must have allowed the energy into his being. When he woke up, nothing was dramatically different, but he felt lighter and had a clearer mind. He told himself that he must have had a good sleep for once and thanked his lucky stars. He had more to thank than his stars.

That evening, Ben met up with Esther for a planned dinner date.

"Why aren't you drinking tonight?" asked Esther.

"I don't know," said Ben.

"Have you decided to have a break from it?" asked Esther, thinking that her influence may have precipitated a good change in Ben's drinking habit.

"No," said Ben. "I haven't decided anything. But ever since I woke up, something in me has changed."

He stared at the empty wine glass and had no desire to fill it. He thought (with a wisdom he had never tasted before), *We drink because we want the happiness that comes with mental oblivion. There is another way. Less damaging, less up and down, more healthy, more stable.*

Looking at Esther, he said, "You have been good to me...."

He stopped. It wasn't really that she had been good to him. Esther did what suited Esther.

He started his sentence again. "Since you have returned from India, we have been seeing each other again. But I don't want to get back together. I shouldn't have done it the first time. I'm not going to do it a second."

Taking offence at Ben's suggestion that something was wrong with choosing her, Esther warned, "I think it's in your best interest...."

"I have done way too many things because it was 'in my best interest,'" said Ben. "I have followed 'my best interest' regarding work, money, and people."

He became still and added, "It's *not* in my best interest at all."

CHAPTER 38
LIFE PLAYS

I n *Waldmeer:*

Not only did Ben leave Esther, but he left his job at the State Ballet and decided to give himself a year off full-time work. He moved to Waldmeer, took over Shambhavi's Waldmeer Warrior's dance class, and bought a house in town. The house was no less than Farkas's old house. Ide was privately selling it for Farkas's estate, which would go to Farkas and Ide's adult child, Lan-Lan.

How deeply and unknowingly we are all connected.

Ben had never met Farkas, Amira, or Gabriel. He barely knew Ide. He had seen her a few times at Waldmeer Warriors when he owned Nanna's House at Store Creek. He had also crossed paths with her at Prana Community, but had never spoken to her. The only one he knew from that generation was Rybert because of stopping at the Wurt Wurt Koort tearooms.

Although he did not know them, Life knows us all and plays with our interconnectedness. Ben was now the owner of the house which began our Waldmeer journey.

Malik was pleased not only to have Ben as his newest employee but also to have him as a new neighbour. Farkas's old house and Malik's house were a few streets from each other.

For all the years Farkas lived in that house, Malik's house had been in his family. His grandfather built it. His mother (Maria) had been raised in it. When his grandparents died, his mother (Amira) moved back into it. Eventually, his mother (Faith) brought him and his siblings from Borderfirma to the Waldmeer house. While his siblings decided to return to Borderfirma, Malik, who had an instinctive feeling for Earth, made his home in Waldmeer.

Malik and Ben would become closely bonded, lifelong friends.

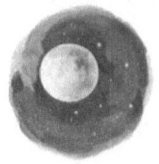

CHAPTER 39
SWEETHEART

ecember Purnima morning, in the Wurt Wurt Koort Tearooms:

D On the morning of December full moon, Merlyn drove to Wurt Wurt Koort to see Rybert.

"Happy Christmas, darling," said Rybert. "One week early, I know. But I won't have time to say it again."

Merlyn kissed him as he walked by, juggling plates.

On his next pass-by, he said, "Guess who is coming to see me this afternoon?"

Each time he passed, he added another piece to the puzzle. "Someone I haven't seen since May." "At my age, seven months is too long to be at odds with someone you love." "He's bringing his new sweetheart." "Benedict. That's his new sweetheart."

"It's Tom," said Merlyn.

She remembered that the last time she had been to Tom & Hardy, her parting words to Tom were, "Just love somebody. Anybody. The next person who walks in the door."

That next person was Benedict, who was indeed a sweetheart.

"If he is ready to make up with you," Merlyn said to Rybert on her way out, "he might be ready to make up with me, too."

"Of course, angel," said Rybert. "It's Christmas."

CHAPTER 40
NO HANDS

December Purnima evening, in Cypress Lane:

D Merlyn could see the shops' Christmas lights swaying in the summer evening breeze. The branches in Cypress Lane moved in sync with them. The grand old trees oscillated their reach between the lit-up shops and the unlit beach. If you sat on the beach long enough, your eyes adjusted to the moonlight. Then, it seemed as lit as the street.

In the distance, Merlyn could see Ben walking towards the pier. He was probably going to watch the full moon with all the holidaymakers. He wasn't a holidaymaker. He was a homemaker. Merlyn hadn't spoken to him since his recent move, but she knew about it through Ide.

Before Merlyn headed back up the hill to home, she decided to have one last walk along Cypress Lane to Waldmeer Boathouse and Cafe, which stood with quiet ease at the end of the dirt road. No one was around. The cafe had closed hours ago. As she sat on its deserted decking, watching the eternally interesting waves, a voice came from the dark lane. It was too black to see more than a moving shadow. Dark or light, she knew that voice.

"Have you been watching the moon?" she asked.

"Yes," said Ben.

"Congratulations," said Merlyn, "on your new house."

He sat next to her on the decking. Neither said anything as they now had the luxury of knowing that time was not of the essence.

"It's getting late," said Ben. "I'll walk you up the hill."

Halfway up, Merlyn said, "You understand that I'm not really partnerable anymore?"

After a moment, Ben replied, "Neither am I."

"No," laughed Merlyn. "You are definitely partnerable. You are just disillusioned. There's a big difference."

Ben shrugged and said, "You don't have to hold my hand. I'm a grown-up."

He watched Merlyn's soft, amused expression. He missed those eyes—eyes born of Earth but belonging to Heaven.

"We'll see," said Merlyn with a mixture of levity and earnestness. "Let's keep walking. No hands."

The moon looked down with the seeming same levity and seriousness as Merlyn's. After you have seen the world come and go many times, some things become deadly serious and others become not worth a second glance.

The moon waxes and wanes
with our passing days.
Yet, despite appearances,
there is no waxing and waning.

It is always full,
always glowing,
always being a complete
and perfect Purnima.

SUMMARY OF WALDMEER SERIES

A multi-generational journey of spiritual awakening, healing, and the spaces between worlds.

Beneath the surface of an idyllic coastal village, unseen forces stir. Waldmeer is a place where the visible and invisible meet—where inter-dimensional realms brush against everyday life, and where emotional truths rise quietly but undeniably.

Told across seven books, the *Waldmeer Series* follows Maria–Amira from the groundedness of her rural home to the doorways into higher realms of perception and spiritual transformation. Around her, those she loves and seeks to help are drawn into their own awakenings, resistances, and reckonings.

Waldmeer moves between ordinary moments and otherworldly initiations. Between earthly love and higher love. Between who we think we are... and what we truly are.

At times tender, at times confronting, these stories unfold in layers—personal, relational, and metaphysical.

ABOUT THE AUTHOR

On the beach at Lorne, Australia (the coastal village Waldmeer is based on).

Donna Goddard is a spiritual author whose work blends clarity, devotion, and metaphysical insight. With 25+ published books across spiritual nonfiction, fiction, poetry, and children's literature, she writes to uplift consciousness and offer healing through words.

Donna's Facebook author page has over 400,000 followers worldwide, and her YouTube channel has received 4 million views. Her books are read by spiritual seekers globally and are known for their honesty, poetic style, and transformative energy.

Her writing is an offering—to help others awaken their own inner spirit, trust its guidance, and create a life of depth, beauty, and quiet joy.

All links at https://linktr.ee/donnagoddard

Ratings and Reviews

Donna would be grateful for any ratings or reviews.

ALSO BY DONNA GODDARD

Fiction

Waldmeer Series: A Spiritual Fiction Series
Nanima Series: Spiritual Fiction
Enanika Series: Visionary Fiction
Riverland Series (children's fiction 6 to 9 years)
Foxie (children's fiction 7 to 12 years)

Nonfiction

Love and Devotion Series
Sweet Spirit Series
Consciousness Series
Being Meditation Series
Many Moments Series
Poetry Series
Love's Longing
Dance: A Spiritual Affair
Writing: A Spiritual Voice